FROZEN IN TIME

A Story About
One Woman's Efforts
To Rebuild A Town
That Was Destroyed By An Earthquake

This is a work of fiction. Similarities to real people, places, or events are entirely coincidental.

FROZEN IN TIME

First edition. November 21, 2024.

Copyright © 2024 VINCENT GILVARRY.

ISBN: 979-8230905493

Written by VINCENT GILVARRY.

Also by VINCENT GILVARRY

Merlin's School for Aspiring Lightworkers
Destiny Calls

Merlin's School of Magic and Mystery
The Thrill of The Unknown

Standalone
I Will Be Praying For Your Soul
Masterminds of Mischief
Fun and Games at The Passionfruit Hotel
Merlin's School of Magic and Mystery
Frozen in Time

Watch for more at https://vgilvarry.blog/.

Table of Contents

Frozen in Time 1
PROLOGUE 3
CHAPTER 1 6
CHAPTER 2 9
CHAPTER 3 12
CHAPTER 4 14
CHAPTER 5 15
CHAPTER 6 18
CHAPTER 7 22
CHAPTER 8 25
CHAPTER 9 28
CHAPTER 10 31
CHAPTER 11 38
CHAPTER 12 40
CHAPTER 13 44
CHAPTER 14 48
CHAPTER 15 49
CHAPTER 16 51
EPILOGUE 53
CHAPTER 17 56

VINCENT GILVARRY

AUTHOR'S COMMENT

This story is a product of my imagination but the setting, the mountain village of Poggioreale is not imaginary. It was one of fourteen towns that was destroyed in the Belice earthquake on the southwest coast of Sicily in 1968.

In this story, a passionate Sicilian woman has an opportunity to do the impossible. And with the help of her family, and numerous other people, she oversees the reconstruction of Poggioreale.

It's a labour of love and a task that is not without its difficulties, and over a period of twenty years, it brings a community together and it brings the village back to life.

The original inhabitants of Poggioreale would happily move back in if someone rebuilt their town, but that will never happen. And like Pompeii, it will be forever frozen in time.

PROLOGUE

A Journey to Safety
From Naples to Poggioreale
Sicily - 1943

Naples was a war-torn city during World War 11, shrouded in fear and uncertainty, a victim of indiscriminate attacks, heavy bombing raids, and countless deaths.

War is an ugly thing and it is more so for the mothers of helpless children. Not knowing what else to do, one desperate mother, Lucia Grasso decided to put her three sons and her five year-old daughter on the night train and send them up into the mountains to stay with her parents.

It was a last minute decision, and they had to race through darkened streets to make it to the train station on time. Little Florentina held onto her mother's hand as they battled their way through the crowd, dodging suitcases and soldiers. "Mama, why are we leaving at night?" she asks, her voice quivering with uncertainty.

Her mother forces a smile, masking the dread in her heart. "Because it's safer, my darling. And, when you get to Nonno's, he will take care of you."

Little Florentina didn't want to go, so Lucia knelt down and held her hands, the look in her eyes was one of anguish and pain, and those last few minutes with her children were filled with tears and a hurried goodbye.

"Florentina, you have to go and stay with Nonno and Nonna, that is why."

Florentina's eyes were filled with tears. "Why can't you come with us, Mama?"

Lucia's face softened, and through trembling lips she forced a reply. "Because it's safer for you in Poggioreale, because I must stay here to help the others."

"What if the bad men come to the mountains?" Florentina cried, as she clutched onto her little dolly.

Her mother's gaze was distilled with fear and determination. "Nonno Pietro will protect you. He is the bravest man I know."

The train was about to depart, and Lucia held her sons and daughter, never knowing if she would ever see them again, her heart breaking with every passing second.

"Remember, my bambini," she says as she takes them in her arms, "you are stronger than you think. And one day, you will understand why I sent you up into the mountains."

She bundled her children onto the carriage, the train doors slammed shut, and Florentina, tears streaming down her cheeks, pressed her face against the window pane, and watched as her mother disappeared into a haze of steam and smoke.

Her brother's did their best to be brave but they had never been on a train before, it was dark, the train jostled from side to side, and the sound of bombs in the distance did little to ease their heartache or their fear.

They were heading up into the mountains, to the village of Poggioreale on the southwest coast of Sicily, where the wind whispered through the olive trees, and the earth was filled with the salty tang of the Mediterranean and the scent of freshly tilled soil.

Nestled at the base of Mount Elimo, Poggioreale, escaped much of the war's cruelty. Its sun-warmed streets remained intact, and its wheatfields and vineyards continued to thrive under the Sicilian sun.

Little Florentina's heart ached for her mother, and she often sat on the wooden bench outside of Nonno Pietro's house while he showed her how to weave a basket.

"Nonno, will the war come here?" she asked, her little voice tinged with fear.

Pietro paused and gazed out across the valley with thoughtful eyes. "No, piccolina," he replied, his voice steady. "This place is protected. The mountains watch over us."

Nonna Lucia was cooking in the kitchen, and the aroma of baking bread filled the air, while Bruno, the shaggy brown dog dozed lazily at her feet, oblivious to the weight of the world outside.

Florentina's arrival in Poggioreale had not been without sorrow. For a little girl, the journey from Naples was horrifying. The train was packed with anxious faces, but she held onto the hands of her brothers who did their best to assure their little sister that they would be safe by morning.

"Why couldn't Mama come with us?" Florentina asked her grandfather.

He brushed the hair out of her eyes and said, "She sent you here so you would be safe, tesoro. The city is no place for a child right now."

As Florentina watched her grandfather work, the rhythm of his hands calmed her nerves. She had no idea at the time that Poggioreale was imprinting itself onto her soul and would continue to do so for the remainder of her life.

It's cobblestone streets overlooked lush vineyards and rolling hills, and Florentina found solace with her grandparents close by. The warmth of Nonna's kitchen, the rhythmic sound of Nonno working with his tools, and a love affair with Bruno the dog were etched into the fabric of her childhood.

Florentina discovered the simple joys of life, picking olives, chasing Bruno and her brothers around the square, and sitting on the porch with Nonno Pietro, who had endless tales of Poggioreale's noble past.

"Do you know, Florentina, that this valley holds secrets," Nonno Pietro said, his eyes glinting in the twilight.

"What sort of secrets?" she had said, her eyes wide.

Nonno Pietro chuckled. "Stories about treasures, and maybe even ghosts, but they only reveal themselves to those who truly belong here."

CHAPTER 1

Naples – 1970
An Unexpected Legacy

It is mid-morning and the bustling back streets of Naples are alive with activity, a chaotic cacophony of people going about their business, women in floral dresses haggling at market stalls, their voices rising in a symphony of determination. Vendors hawk their wares, and the aroma of espresso mingles with the briny breeze that floats in from the harbour.

A vibrant, thirty-two year-old woman called Florentina Grasso strides confidently through the crowd minding her own business. But when you are dressed like a popular movie, the men not only notice, some of them can barely restrain themselves.

"Ciao, bella," says a godlike young creature called Vito, as he leans nonchalantly against a fruit stand with a grin as wide as his ambitions are narrow.

"Where are you going in such a hurry? Stay and talk to me."

Florentina usually smiles and sometimes she even shares her thoughts rather loudly and vividly. She does her best to ignore the likes of Vito and Rico, gigolos in tight-fitting shirts and cheap plastic sunglasses. They hang about doing nothing and specialise in wolf whistles and insinuations. Florentina throws him a look that says never in a million years and laughs.

"Why would I waste my time on someone as gorgeous as you?"

"Bella, I love you, and I want to marry you?" Rico says. "And where are you going?'

Florentina doesn't even break her stride but responds, nevertheless.

"Somewhere that your brain won't understand."

Florentina is a woman on a mission, and today, she is dressed in a sky blue dress with pencil thin shoulder straps, a revealing but closely fitted bodice, a belt of the same colour, and a skirt that billows out just above the knees.

She is the proprietor of a successful dress shop that caters to a very different clientele, but Florentina turns heads as easily as her piercing eyes can silence a catcall. She knows the power of appearances and wields it like a sword.

Vito and Rico burst into laughter but Florentina has already gone, her heels clicking against the cobblestones as she approaches the door of Salvatore Donato's office.

The peeling paint and cracked shutters hint at the city's wear and tear, but a polished brass plaque on the door gleams with dignity. The façade of the building belies the sleek modernity of the office, and of the man within.

A cool breeze wafts through the window of Salvatore Donato's office and it is mercifully free of tobacco smoke, a rarity in Naples, but it is on the top floor of a building that is in desperate need of a fresh coat of paint.

Salvatore is an amiable man in his sixties with clear blue eyes and perfectly manicured silver grey hair who wears a black suit and gold rimmed eye glasses.

He greets Florentina with a warm smile, and a kiss on both cheeks.

"Signorina Grasso, it is always a pleasure," he says, "and today, you look majestical as usual."

"Thank you," she says. "Appearances may be superficial, but they should never be underestimated."

"Indeed," he says. "Please take a seat."

Florentina does so and places her handbag carefully on her lap. "I hope this isn't going to take long," she says.

Salvatore chuckles and adjusts his gold-rimmed spectacles. "Straight to business, as always. An admirable trait, but this is not a small matter. It's about your grandfather's will."

Florentina's sharp gaze softens. "Nonno Pietro? What about his will?"

"I assure you that I will be efficient, but I must warn you that what you are about to hear may surprise you."

The minutes stretch on, his voice steady as he mentions a few details. And when he reaches the part about her inheritance, Florentina catches her breath.

"Nonno left me the village of Poggioreale," she says, incredulously.

Salvatore nods. "Your grandfather was a man of mystery it seems. He purchased Poggioreale after the earthquake, though no one knew, and now, it's yours."

Florentina leans back, her mind whirling. She had expected nothing more than a few keepsakes, perhaps a token gesture from her beloved Nonno Pietro but an entire town and a ghost town at that.

"He left me an entire town," she says. "Is this some kind of joke?"

Salvatore shakes his head. "Not at all. It seems that your grandfather purchased the village after the earthquake, and no one knew anything about it, until now."

Florentina sits back, her mind racing. Poggioreale, the village that she had once called home was destroyed by an earthquake a year before.

"Why would he leave it to me?"

Salvatore smiles gently. "Perhaps because you meant so much to him, or perhaps because he saw something in you that others didn't."

On that day, in Salvatore Donato's office, Florentina's life changes. A revelation of such a magnitude is almost too incredible to believe.

"I am sorry, this does say an entire town, doesn't it?" she says, as she leans forward hoping to hear more.

"Yes, signorina. It's all true and it is now yours," he says.

Florentina, usually so focused can hardly even think. She thanks Salvatore, places the will in her handbag and heads for the streets.

As she navigates the crowd with purpose, her sky-blue dress, cinched at the waist sways as she walks. Heads turn as she passes, some with admiration, and others with envy. Florentina ignores them all, her focus is set on the envelope in her handbag, and unfortunately, she encounters Vito and Rico on the return journey, both of whom are still up to their old tricks.

"Bella, marry me please," Vito cries.

"Not today or any other day," Florentina replies, not even breaking her stride.

"Hey, Rico, did you hear that?" Vito says. "She loves me."

"Dream on, Vito," he replies, laughing loudly.

Florentina rolls her eyes and mutters under her breath, "Idioti."

Just before she gets back to her shop, Florentina stops and glances up at the clear blue sky. The summer sun is warm on her face, and as she feels the weight of her grandfather's legacy settle on her shoulders, she has a feeling that her life really is about to change forever.

CHAPTER 2

Poggioreale: A Ghost Town

Florentina told her staff and family that she had to go on a business trip to northern Sicily, but her true destination lays to the south, Poggioreale, a place frozen in time and memory.

She boards the night train at the station, the deeds to the town safely secured in her handbag like a secret too big to hold. The train's rhythmic clatter fills the compartment as it makes its way through the darkened night.

Florentina gazes out the window, her thoughts as turbulent as the shifting landscape, her reflection appearing and disappearing every few seconds against passing headlights and house lights.

Rolling hills dotted with cypress trees give way to distant mountains, and the scent of wild herbs seep in through the cracks of the carriage, but her thoughts are as restless as the rattling sounds of the noisy old train.

The journey stretches on from night to day but Florentina has made this journey countless times before. The train hisses to a stop in the nearest town, where she disembarks and boards an early morning bus that will take her up to Poggioreale. The rickety old bus sways precariously as it winds its way along the narrow mountain road, and when Poggioreale finally comes into view, it is but a silhouette against the pale light of morning.

From a distance, it looks untouched but as the bus draws closer, the truth is revealed. Crumbling walls, overgrown pathways, and silence hangs over the village like a ghostly memory, casting long, eerie shadows.

As Florentina steps off the bus, the driver gives her a curious look but says nothing as he pulls away. She has not been here since her grandfather's funeral, and now, she is returning, not as a guest but as its owner.

The village she remembers is now a skeleton of its former self, with debris where houses once stood. She makes her way up the familiar path to her grandfather's house, her footsteps echoing in the stillness.

By some miracle or other, it survived, a stubborn relic against time. Her childhood memories are everywhere, on the old stone well where she and Nonna used to draw water, and under the fig tree where Bruno chased shadows, but now, it all seems so much smaller, and is shrouded in decay.

The old wooden door creaks and a wave of nostalgia washes over Florentina as soon as she steps inside the house. The air is cool and scented with the herbs that her grandfather hung out to dry. The kitchen table has four small chairs, the fireplace is spotlessly clean, and on the windowsill is a small clay pot that still holds the remains of a basil plant.

The envelope that she came to find is where Salvatore said it would be, hidden behind the old clock on the mantelpiece. Its edges are yellowed and the ink is still legible, but beside it is another envelope, and a package wrapped in brown paper tied up with string.

Florentina takes a seat on the porch and gazes out at the landscape where the morning sun paints the valley in green and gold, and with trembling hands, she unfolds and reads the letter.

Cara Florentina, if you are reading this, then I have already left this world, and you have returned to Poggioreale. Even though I am no longer here to welcome you, this place has always been your home, just as you have always been its heart.

You were the only one who ever came to visit, and the only one who ever listened to my stories. This town, this piece of our family history now belongs to you, not just because you are my granddaughter, but because you cared.

In the tunnels beneath the church, you will find the treasures left behind by the noble families of Poggioreale, all of whom passed away a very long time ago.

This town holds secrets, treasures of its past that I have kept safe for years. They belong to you now, not just the riches in the tunnels, but the spirit of Poggioreale itself. Guard it well, and it will give you a purpose greater than you can imagine. What you do with the treasures is your decision, but I know that you will think of something worthwhile.

Your loving grandfather, Nonno Pietro.

Tears well in Florentina's eyes as she holds the letter to her heart. Her grandfather's faith feels like a blessing and a burden. The second letter is a map that show a series of tunnels beneath the town, and the package contains a heavy iron key, its ornate design a testament to another era.

Florentina stares out across the valley, her thoughts racing. Do those tunnels really contain treasures? The enormity of her grandfather's trust weighs on her heart, mind and soul. She came seeking answers but will leave with more questions.

Nonno holds a special place in her heart, and she obviously held a special place in his, but what she will do with this place she has no idea.

CHAPTER 3

Exploring the Past

Florentina spends the morning exploring the ruins of Poggioreale. The air is crisp and carries the faint hum of cicadas. She climbs over rubble where houses once stood, their remnants covered in moss and wildflowers, a poignant reminder that life once thrived in this beautiful little town.

A stray cat darts between the ruins, the only sign of life. The map in Florentina's hand leads to the old church at the centre of the village. Chiesa Madre Di Poggioreale was located in Piazza Elimo and stood at the top of a series of stone steps on the upper edge of the town. The roof has caved in but the facade and some of the bell tower survived.

The heavy oak doors are no longer there and no longer groan but shafts of sunlight stream through broken stained-glass windows that cast fragmented rainbows on the floor.

Armed with the map and the key, Florentina sets out to find the tunnels. The church is a shell of its former self, its roof partially collapsed and its once-vivid frescoes faded.

The entrance to the tunnels is supposed to be behind the altar, and after searching around she finds the trapdoor beneath a loose slab of stone, its hinges rusted but functional. With a deep breath, she inserts the key and the lock opens with ease.

The hinges creak as she lifts the door, revealing a steep, narrow staircase that descends into the darkness, the air cool and damp. Florentina lights one of Nonno's oil lamps, and the flame casts a flickering shadow on the walls. The tunnels smell of earth and age, the stone walls etched with markings she cannot decipher.

Her heart races as she ventures deeper. The first chamber is small and lined with wooden crates and shelves covered in dust. She opens one of the crates and gasps. Inside are gilded frames, and paintings of aristocrats in elaborate attire, while another crate contains porcelain figurines, their delicate features unmarred by time.

The second chamber is larger, its walls lined with shelves that hold books, ledgers, and bundles of letters tied with ribbons. In the centre of the room stands a chest, its lid slightly ajar. Inside she finds velvet pouches filled with jewels, emeralds, rubies, and pearls that sparkle in the lamplight.

Florentina opens an ornate wooden box, only to discover a delicate silver necklace, its pendant shaped like a rose. She holds it up to the light, marvelling at its craftsmanship. The necklace seems to whisper of the woman who once wore it, her story now lost to history.

But the tunnels are not without danger. One section has partially collapsed, the stones unstable under her feet. As Florentina ventures deeper, she hears a faint rumbling and dust rains from the ceiling. She hurries back the way she came, her heart pounding.

Emerging into the daylight, she sits on the steps of the church, clutching more anxiety than memories. The treasures are real, but they come with a stark reminder: Poggioreale's past was fragile and so was its future.

The treasures were hidden away long before the earthquake ever destroyed the town, but they are also items of value and are probably worth a small fortune. An idea is formulating in her mind and a smile plays on her lips for the first time since leaving Salvatore's office.

"This is going to take a while," she says, her mind buzzing with possibilities.

"Nonno left me more than an inheritance; he entrusted me with a legacy."

"I will figure it out, Nonno," she whispers to the wind. "I will do right by you."

CHAPTER 4

A Decision Has Been Made

Florentina sits on the porch of her grandfather's house, staring out across the valley as the evening sun dips low in the sky. The absence of noise in Poggioreale is profound, unlike the constant hum of Naples. Here, time is suspended, the air carrying the soft rustle of the wind through the olive groves.

The treasures weigh on her mind. They are not just riches, they are the relics of a forgotten era, of a town that had once bustled with life. Her grandfather's words echo in her ears: *What you do with them is your decision, but I know that you will think of something worthwhile.*

Florentina closes her eyes and imagines the Poggioreale of her childhood. The laughter of the villagers, the scent of freshly baked bread wafting from the kitchens, the colourful markets where she used to run and play. The town was alive then, vibrant with community and tradition.

A memory surfaces of her Nonna Lucia teaching her to knead dough in their kitchen. "A good loaf," Nonna had said, "is like a home, it needs love, care, and time to rise."

Florentina opens her eyes and a decision has been made. She will restore Poggioreale, not just for herself, but for the memory of those who once lived here and for those who might return.

"It won't be easy but Nonno believed in me. That has to mean something."

The first step is to convince her brothers of this plan. And while they have always been sceptical of her whims, Florentina knows that she cannot do this alone.

CHAPTER 5

Rallying the Family

She returns to Naples two days later, the noise of the city hitting her like a wave after the stillness of Poggioreale. She is about to meet her brothers Antonio, Marco, and Luca in a small trattoria not far from her dress shop.

The three men are already seated when she arrives, their conversation animated. Antonio, the eldest, is stern and pragmatic, his shirt neatly pressed. Marco, the middle brother is more laid-back, his sleeves rolled up and his tie loose. Luca, the youngest has always had a mischievous glint in his eyes and enjoys life too much to take it seriously.

"Ah, la nostra sorellina," Antonio says as he greets his sister and gives her a kiss on each cheek.

Luca leans back in his chair, curious as to what this is all about. "If this is another one of your grand schemes sorellina, I'm in. Just say the word."

"But tell us quickly, what is this mysterious meeting all about?"

Florentina can't help but smile. Luca has always been her ally, his boundless optimism a welcome counterpoint to Antonio's practicality.

"This," she says as she places an envelope on the table. "This is the deed to Poggioreale."

The brothers exchange puzzled glances. Marco opens the envelope and scans the document before passing it onto Antonio.

Luca leans forward, curiosity sparking in his eyes. "Now, you really do have to tell us everything."

Her brothers listen with varying degrees of belief and disbelief as Florentina explains the contents of the will and the fact that Nonno Pietro left her a fortune in treasures that are hidden in tunnels under the church.

"He left you an entire town and treasures as well?" Antonio says. "Florentina, this sounds fantastical."

"It's real, Antonio, and I have seen it with my own eyes. But it's more than just a treasure. It's history. Nonno believed in preserving it for the future, but I want to do the impossible."

"And what's that?"

"I want to rebuild Poggioreale."

Antonio's brow furrows. "Poggioreale is a ghost town. Why would you want anything to do with it now?"

"It is not about what I want," Florentina replies, her tone steady. "Nonno Pietro left it to me to decide what I want to do with the treasure. He believed that Poggioreale could be saved, and I think he was right."

Marco shakes his head. "Do you have any idea how much work that would take? The place is in ruins."

"Exactly," Antonio says. "And it's not just the physical restoration. There are permits, bureaucratic red tape, and the costs would be astronomical."

Luca leans forward, grinning. "Ah, but think of the potential. A beautiful, historic town brought back to life. Tourists would come from everywhere just to see it."

"And who's going to pay for this?" Antonio wants to know, as he glares at Luca. "You? With what money?"

Florentina raises a hand and silences them. "That treasure is worth a fortune and it will pay for the restoration."

The discussion continues for nearly an hour. Antonio points out every possible pitfall, Marco raises logistical concerns, and Luca makes light of the whole thing. But as Florentina describes her vision, the square and church restored, a new vineyard, a museum to showcase Poggioreale's history, their resistance starts to waver.

"Tell us more about this treasure," Marco says.

"The tunnels are filled with artifacts, jewels, paintings, and heirlooms, which is more than enough to restore the town and then some."

Antonio leans back, his arms crossed. "If this is true, and I'm not saying it isn't, you are risking everything. Do you really think you can pull this off?"

Florentina meets his gaze. "I don't think I can Antonio. I know I will, but I can't do it alone. I need your help."

Antonio crosses his arms. "Why us?"

"Because we are family," she replies. "And because I can't do it alone. Marco, you are good with logistics. Luca, you know people, tradesmen and suppliers. And Antonio, you will keep us grounded. Together, we will make this happen."

There's a long silence as her words settle in their minds. Finally, Luca grins. "Well, it sounds like an adventure. Count me in," he says as he raises his coffee cup in a mock toast. "Let's resurrect a ghost town."

"But you need a solid plan," Marco says. "I can't believe I am saying this, but you can count me in too. Someone has to keep this operation running smoothly."

All eyes turn to Antonio who sighs heavily. "This is madness, but Nonno was a good man, and if he believed in this idea, then, I suppose I can too."

"But if you are going to do this Florentina, you will need someone to deal with the bureaucrats and I suppose that's me."

Florentina's smile is radiant. "Thank you, I knew that I could count on you. And I promise that I will think of a nice way to repay you, in about twenty years' time."

CHAPTER 6

The First Steps

A few weeks later, a convoy of trucks and quite a few members of the Grasso family arrive in Poggioreale. The crisp mountain air is invigorating but they are shocked at what they see. They stand in silence at the edge of the town as they try to come to terms with a place they all knew and loved.

As they look around, it's a sobering sight. The once-vibrant town is now a ghost of its former self, its empty streets echoing with the memories of a bygone era.

For Florentina, this is a bittersweet reminder of the joys of childhood, coupled with the enormity of the task ahead. For her brothers, it's a wake-up call to realise just how ambitious their sister's dream really is.

"This is what you want to rebuild?" Marco says.

Florentina shoots him a determined look.

"Not just rebuild, Marco, but restore."

Luca chuckles and slaps Marco on the back.

"In that case, I guess we'll need a few more hammers," he says.

Antonio remains silent, his arms crossed as he surveys the scene, but they can't stand around admiring the scenery as they have a lot to do before the real work starts. Everyone pitches in to erect tents and shelters as close to Nonno Pietro's place as possible.

When the Grasso family gets together, it is usually something to celebrate, but their mother Lucia, and their father Paulo, who are both hale and hearty and in their mid-sixties were not about to left out and offer to be chief cooks and bottle washers.

A night of subdued celebration and of reflection follows, but the next day is one to look forward to as they will finally get too see the hidden treasure.

Everyone gathers around as Florentina places the map on the table.

"This," she says, as she taps the map, "is where we start. We have to remove the treasure from the tunnels, find a place to store them, and then work out how to sell them for the best price."

"But some of the tunnels are dangerous and we will have to be very careful."

"If I remember correctly," Luca says, "Nonno had a wine cellar under his house. We could store them there."

"I had completely forgotten about that," Florentina says. "Let's go and check it out."

Beneath the modest yet sturdy walls of Nonno Pietro's house is a wine cellar that could be as old as Poggioreale itself. The entrance is concealed beneath a heavy wooden trapdoor in the kitchen, its iron hinges rusty but still strong. A faint scent of earth and aged oak wafts up when the door is opened and mingles with the aroma of the house above.

As they descend the narrow stone staircase, the air grows cooler, laden with the tang of damp stone and fermented grapes. The cellar has been carved into the rocky foundations of the house, its walls uneven but timeless, bearing the marks of hand tools that were in use decades ago, perhaps even centuries, ago.

A kerosine lamps hangs from the ceiling, and numerous candles in candleholders hint of a time long past when Pietro and Lucia would sit around and share a bottle of wine in the flickering light.

Wooden racks line the walls, sagging slightly under the weight of glass bottles sealed with wax. Each bottle bears a handwritten label, its ink faded but legible, detailing the vintage year and the type of grape.

"Look at all of this," Luca says. "Nero d'Avola, Catarratto, Zibibbo. We won't run short of wine, that's for sure."

Some bottles are covered in a thin layer of dust but they are relics of another age, and some gleam as if Pietro had cleaned them only recently.

At the centre of the room is a rough-hewn wooden table, its surface scarred with decades of use. Scattered across the top are remnants of Pietro's meticulous work: a corking device, a collection of tasting glasses, and a ledger filled with neat, looping handwriting.

"This is a chronicle of Poggioreale's bounty, detailing harvests, weather patterns, and notes on flavour profiles," Antonio says. "Nonno was very meticulous, wasn't he?"

In one corner, they find quite a few empty barrels, their wood dark with age and stained where wine had once seeped through.

"That's where we should store the treasure," Marco says.

The scent is intoxicating, a blend of oak, fruit, and time itself. In one corner of the room are Pietro's tools: a tasting ladle, a grape press, and a rusted pair of pruning shears, each carefully placed as though waiting for him to return. And despite its age and simplicity, the cellar radiates warmth and care.

"This isn't just a place for storing wine," Paulo says, "it's a sanctuary where Nonno Pietro poured his heart and soul into preserving Poggioreale's legacy, one bottle at a time."

For Florentina, this discovery is like unearthing a piece of her grandfather's soul, a tangible reminder of the love and passion that shaped her family and their home.

This cellar is not merely a storage space but a bridge to the past, a place where history, love, and the essence of Poggioreale have been distilled into liquid memory.

They spend the remainder of the day transferring the wooden crates with the gilded frames, as well as the porcelain figurines, the books, ledgers, and letters, but the chest of jewels proves to be another matter altogether.

"That weighs a ton," Marco says. "How are we going to move that thing through the tunnels and then down into Nonno's cellar?"

"I think we should do so very carefully." Lucia says.

"Each of us could wear some of those things," Luca says."

And for the next few hours, they wander back and forth carrying and wearing rings, necklaces, and an assortment of other fabulous jewels, embedded with emeralds, rubies, and pearls.

Florentina shows everyone the ornate wooden box that contains the silver necklace with a rose shaped pendant.

"Mama, I think you should have this," she says.

Lucia barely knows what to think but accepts the gift gracefully.

"All of this will fund the work we want to do and that's the good part," Florentina says,.

"And the bad part?" Luca says.

"We have to clear away the debris and then decide which structures we can salvage."

Marco's, logistical mind is already working overtime. "We will need help, like local tradesmen, masons, labourer's and permits, don't forget those."
Antonio grumbles. "Permits means dealing with officials. That won't be easy."
"I will handle them," Florentina says firmly. "I have dealt with worse in Naples."
The family spend the rest of the day touring the town, taking notes and discussing ideas. Florentina's vision is about to take shape: cobblestone streets, restored villas, a vibrant marketplace, and vineyards which will thrive once again on the surrounding hillside.

CHAPTER 7

Bureaucratic Battles

Back in Naples, Florentina begins the gruelling task of navigating the bureaucratic maze. Her first stop is the municipal office in Palermo, one in which the smell of stale coffee and bureaucracy is thicker than the air.

She has been waiting for hours to speak with Signor Vizzini, the official in charge of granting permits for historical restorations.

Antonio, ever the pragmatist, had warned her that this would not be easy, but nothing could have prepared her for a condescending man with a perpetually sour expression and an air of self-importance.

Vizzini is in his sixties, with slicked-back hair and the kind of smile that says he has already made up his mind. He toys with a pen as Florentina outlines her plans for Poggioreale, her tone measured but firm.

Vizzini leans back in his chair and examines the papers that Florentina has placed before him.

"You want to rebuild Poggioreale?" he says, incredulous. "A ghost town?"

"The town has historical significance, and this restoration project could bring tourism and economic growth to the region."

Florentina keeps her tone polite but firm. "I want to restore it, and yes, I am here to ensure that everything is done properly."

"Properly?" Vizzini snorts. "Signorina, do you have any idea how many permits this will require? Environmental assessments, historical preservation approvals, and zoning regulations, just to start with."

Florentina interrupts, her voice sharp.

"I have done my research, Signor Vizzini. I know exactly what's required, and I have already started gathering the necessary documentation. Now, if you would like to discuss specific concerns, I will be happy to address them."

Vizzini pretends to feign interest. "Tourism, you say, and you expect me to believe that a ghost town will suddenly become a hub of activity?"

"It is already happening," she replies. "The museum and the vineyard restoration is underway, and all I need are the permits for the next phase."

Vizzini taps his pen on the desk. "Permits are tricky, Signorina Grasso. There are environmental assessments to consider, zoning regulations, and these things take time."

Florentina's jaw tightens. "As I have said, I have already submitted the necessary paperwork. The delays seem to be ridiculously excessive."

Vizzini's smile sharpens. "Excessive? You must understand, these processes cannot be rushed. But perhaps if you were to make a contribution to expedite things, we could move forward."

Her eyes narrowed. "A contribution, you mean a bribe, don't you?"

"A donation," he says smoothly. "To support the council's efforts. Surely you understand."

Florentina gets to her feet and kicks the chair to the side. "What I understand, Signor Vizzini, is that Poggioreale deserves better than to be held hostage by red tape and bribery. If you do not approve the permits, then I will find someone who will."

Vizzini is taken aback by her confidence and clears his throat. "Well, I suppose we can begin the process, but don't expect it to be quick."

Florentina smiles, her eyes flashing. "I don't expect quick, Signor Vizzini. I expect thorough, and I will be monitoring this routine every step of the way."

His smirk falters for a moment. "Good luck, Signorina. You will need it."

Back in Poggioreale, Florentina's frustration is palpable as she recounts the meeting to her brothers. Antonio listens in stony silence, and Marco and Luca pace the room, muttering curses under their breath.

"This is exactly what I warned you about," Antonio said. "Vizzini isn't going to budge unless you play his game."

"And you think I should?" Florentina snaps back. "I am not handing over money to a corrupt bureaucrat."

"I am not saying you should," Antonio replies, his voice rising. "But we need to be realistic. Without those permits, this project is dead in the water."

Marco interjects, his tone calmer. "What if we go around him? Find someone higher up who can override his decisions?"

"That's exactly what I am going to do. I have heard about a woman called Bianca Morretti who has connections in the preservation community. She might know how to help."

Luca, leaning against the wall, smirks. "Let me guess, Bianca's the one with the sensible shoes and the 'no-nonsense' look?"

Florentina shoots him a withering glare, but she can't suppress a smile. "Yes, Luca, and I think she is the one who can save this project."

Over the following weeks, Florentina juggles meetings with officials, consultations with architects, and calls to potential investors. Her brothers work tirelessly in Poggioreale, coordinating cleanup efforts and scouting around for tradesmen who are willing to take on the challenge.

One evening, after the sun dips below the horizon, Marco introduces Florentina to a mason named Carlo Ricci, a tall, broad-shouldered man with a quiet strength that immediately catches her attention.

"Signorina Grasso," he says, as he extends a hand. His voice is warm and his handshake is firm.

"Call me Florentina," she replies, her smile genuine.

Carlo is a skilled craftsman with a deep respect for historical architecture, and as they discuss plans for restoring the church, Florentina finds herself drawn to his thoughtful insights.

"This town has history," Carlo says, as he runs his hand over the weathered stone of the church. "And it deserves to be remembered and not forgotten."

"That's exactly why I am doing this," Florentina says. "Poggioreale was my home and it still is."

Their connection grows as they work together, their shared vision for the town intertwining with an undeniable spark of something more.

CHAPTER 8

The Town Awakens

The debris-strewn streets are cleared, revealing cobblestones that have not seen sunlight for over a year, and Poggioreale is gradually coming back to life. The damaged buildings are now scaffolds of hope, their skeletons propped up by the labour of masons, carpenters, and local workers.

Florentina stands in the middle of the square, her hands on her hips. It is noon and the workers have paused for a meal under the shade of a makeshift tent. She watches as Marco coordinates with a supplier, while Luca jokes with the labourers, and Antonio meticulously examines blueprints.

Carlo is inspecting the façade of what had once been the town hall, his brow furrowed in concentration. Florentina approaches and brushes the dust off her shirt.

"You look worried," she says.

Carlo turns, his face softening. "It's not worry, just focus. This wall has cracks that go deeper than I thought. And if we don't reinforce it properly, it won't hold."

"Can it be saved?" Florentina says, hopefully.

"Yes, with time and patience and the right materials," Carlo says. "But it will test us."

"Good," she says. "This town has been through worse and so have we."

The days blend into weeks, and Florentina immerses herself in every detail of the project, from overseeing workers to negotiating with officials. Challenges arise on a daily basis, delayed deliveries, sudden downpours that turn the roads to mud, and bureaucrats who seem to delight in complicating the process.

One afternoon, Antonio arrives with bad news.

"The council is holding up our permits for the restoration of the vineyard," he says, as he tosses his clipboard onto the table where Florentina is reviewing costs.

"Why?" she says, her voice sharp.

"They are claiming that it's an environmental risk," Antonio says.
"It has been farmland for centuries," she says.
"It's an excuse, Florentina. "They want a bribe."
Her jaw tightens. "No, I won't play their game."
"And if they refuse?" he says.
"Then we go higher, to the regional office, and to the media if we must. This project is bigger than their greed."
The siblings rally and write letters and make phone calls. Florentina even visits Palermo herself, her fiery determination breaking through layers of red tape. In the end, the permits are approved, though not without a fight.
As the weeks turn to months, she and Carlo find themselves spending more time together, often under the guise of work, discussing restoration plans, and inspecting progress, but their conversations grow increasingly personal.
One evening, after a long day, Carlo invites her to join him on the steps of the church. He places a glass of wine in her hands and they sit in comfortable silence, the stars above bright against the inky blue sky.
"You are not like anyone I have ever met before," Carlo says, as he breaks the ice.
Florentina raises an eyebrow. "Is that a compliment?" she says.
He chuckles. "Most people would have run a mile as soon as they saw it."
"I couldn't give up. This place is more than just a town to me, it's home."
Carlo's expression is thoughtful. "I think I understand that. A place isn't just bricks and stone, it is memories and stories and you are giving that back to that back to the town."
Their eyes meet, and for a moment, the weight of the day lifts, replaced by something lighter and warmer.
Their relationship deepens in the weeks that follow, and Carlo becomes her confidant, the person she turn to when the pressures of the project feel overwhelming. He, in turn, finds inspiration in her unyielding passion.
One night, a violent storm sweeps through the valley. The workers had secured most of the site, but the wind howls and the rain pours down in torrents. Florentina is at her grandfather's house and pacing anxiously hen there's a knock at the door. She opens it up, only to find Carlo drenched but grinning.
"I thought you might need company," he says.
"Come in before you catch your death," she replies.

They spend the evening by the fire, sharing stories. Carlo speaks of his childhood, of his father who taught him to be a mason, of the pride he feels in working with his hands. Florentina shares her memories of Poggioreale, and her dreams of what it could become.

By the time the storm has passed, their bond has grown stronger, and their partnership solidifies not just in work but in their hearts.

CHAPTER 9

The First Triumph
And
Opposition and Opportunity

One day rolls into another, and everyone is usually up at dawn enjoying breakfast and a warm gentle breeze that carries the scent of freshly turned earth and wildflowers. Florentina gazes out over the square, watching, as the workers put the final touches to Poggioreale's first restored building: the church.

Its stone façade gleams, its once-crumbling walls are now sturdy, and the stained-glass windows have been lovingly restored by artisans.

Curiosity and excitement fills the air as the residents who once called Poggioreale home gather for the unveiling. Florentina feels a swelling of pride and a tinge of nervousness as she addresses the crowd.

"My grandfather, Pietro Grasso, believed in this town. He believed in its history, its people, and its future. Today, we honour that belief by taking the first step toward bringing Poggioreale back to life."

The crowd applauds and the doors of the church are opened to reveal its refurbished interior. Candles flicker on the altar, and the pews, once splintered and broken are now glistening, polished and welcoming.

Inside, the priest gives his blessings, his words resounding through the air. Florentina sits near the back with her brothers, in a state of a quiet satisfaction. Carlo joins her after the service, his eyes warm with approval.

"You have done something incredible," he says.

"And it's just the beginning," Florentina replies, her smile soft but determined.

The celebration that follows spills over into the square, with tables laden with food and wine, laughter and music fill the air, and for the first time in years, Poggioreale feels alive again.

The restoration is a triumph but the momentum is building. Her brothers work tirelessly to organize the next few projects, a community hall, the main street, and the first of the vineyards, but not everyone shares her enthusiasm.

The regional council, stung by Florentina's determination and refusal to play by their rule pushes back. Bureaucratic delays slow the next phase of permits, and whispers of resistance grow louder among sceptical locals.

Florentina sits across from Signor Vizzini once again, this time in the council chambers.

"You have had your little victory," he says, his tone dismissive. "And restoring a church is one thing, but restoring an entire town? That is impossible, Signorina Grasso."

"It is not," Florentina says firmly. "It is progress. Poggioreale has a future, and whether or not you support it, I will find a way."

Vizzini leans back, smirking. "You are persistent, I will give you that, but persistence does not guarantee success."

"Neither does complacency," she shoots back. "And you are one of the most complacent people I have ever met."

The meeting ends without resolution, but Florentina refuses to let his resistance deter her plans. She reaches out to journalists to share the story of Poggioreale's revival. And it's not long before articles about the restoration appear in regional papers, sparking interest from investors and artisans eager to be part of the project.

One morning, a journalist who introduces himself as Giovanni Russo, a writer for a prominent Sicilian magazine arrives in Poggioreale with a camera slung over his shoulder.

"I have heard about what you are doing here," Giovanni says, as he gestures to the restored church and the scaffolding on the nearby buildings.

"And I would like to tell your story."

Florentina agrees and gives him a tour of the town and of her vision. The resulting article paints Poggioreale as a symbol of resilience, a testament to the power of one woman's determination.

Meanwhile, Florentina and Carlo grow closer, their partnership strengthening both professionally and personally. Carlo is her rock, and he always has a solution whenever problems arise.

One evening, as they sit on the porch of her grandfather's house, Florentina confides in him.

"Sometimes I wonder if I am in over my head," she says, her voice tinged with doubt.

Carlo takes her hand, his touch steady.

"You are not. Look at what you have already done. You are building something that will outlast all of us."

She looks at him, her resolve softening. "I just hope it's enough."

The next few months bring tangible successes. The community hall is completed and is the scene of gatherings and celebrations. The first vineyard is replanted and new rows of vines promise a future harvest.

Locals began to trickle back into Poggioreale, drawn by the promise of work and the vision of a restored home. The town, once a ghostly shadow begins to hum with life again.

Meanwhile, Florentina's brothers are discussing more ambitious plans, they want to open an inn or a marketplace for tourists. The possibilities are endless, but Florentina remains focused on one goal, she is going to honour her grandfather's legacy and ensure the survival of Poggioreale.

CHAPTER 10

An Unwelcome Visitor

Word of Poggioreale's restoration is spreading, and inevitably, that includes people with their own agenda. One crisp autumn morning, Florentina finds herself face-to-face with a man who embodies the kind of trouble she has always hoped to avoid. Domenico Bellini steps out of a sleek black car that seems comically out of place against the rustic backdrop.

Florentina is in the square, discussing restoration plans with Carlo, when Domenico approaches. Dressed in a tailored suit and wearing an easy smile, he exudes confidence and an undercurrent of danger.

Domenico is a developer with a reputation for turning quaint villages into soulless tourist hubs. He saunters up to Florentina and extends a hand with a smile that is all charm and no warmth.

"Signorina Grasso," he says smoothly. "I have heard so much about your little project here."

Florentina hesitates before shaking his hand.

"And you are who?" she says.

"Domenico Bellini," he replies. "I represent a group of investors who are very interested in Poggioreale. With the right funding, it could become a premier tourist destination."

"We could turn this quaint little village into a world-class destination. Think of the possibilities, luxury hotels, fine dining, perhaps even a spa, and maybe even a golf course."

Florentina's expression hardens. "Poggioreale is not for sale."

Domenico's smile doesn't falter. "Everything is for sale, signorina. The question is the price."

Carlo steps forward, his expression hard. "This isn't that kind of project."

Domenico glances at Carlo, his smile never wavering. "Ah, of course. You are restoring history. Very noble, but let me be clear, Signorina Grasso: history doesn't pay the bills. Tourism does."

"Poggioreale isn't for sale," Florentina says firmly. "Now, if you will excuse me, I have work to do."

Carlo steps forward, his presence a quiet warning. "I think you have misunderstood. This is not just a business opportunity; this is her home."

"Ah, of course. Sentimentality has its place, but imagine the possibilities, Signorina Grasso. Think of what you could achieve with our resources."

"I do not need your resources," Florentina says firmly. "This town is not a blank canvas for someone else's vision. It has history and I intend to honour that."

Domenico's charm cracks only to reveal a hint of annoyance, and for the briefest moment, it is replaced by a flicker of cold calculation.

"Very well but I will leave my card, just in case you change your mind."

As he walks away, Florentina feels a cold knot of resolve settle in her chest. She knows men like Domenico and they are persistent. She steels herself for whatever will come next.

She turns to Carlo, her voice low but resolute. "He is not going to give up, is he?"

"No," he says. "But neither are we."

Domenico's visit is not the only surprise that the season had in store. As Poggioreale continues its transformation, Florentina's efforts draw the attention of an influential figure in Sicily's cultural heritage sector. Signora Bianca Morretti is an archaeologist and a preservationist with a passion for historical revival.

One morning, she arrives unannounced, and steps out of a modest car with a notebook in hand and an air of authority. She finds Florentina in the vineyard, supervising the planting of new vines.

"You must be Florentina Grasso," she says, her voice firm with eyes that hold a glint of warmth.

Florentina says, "I am and you are who?"

"Bianca Morretti. I work with the regional council on historical preservation. I have heard about what you are doing here, and I must say that I am impressed."

Florentina raises an eyebrow. "The council has not exactly been supportive."

Bianca smiles wryly. "Not all of us are blind to the importance of places like this. I came to see for myself, and I would like to help."

The two women spend the day touring Poggioreale, with Florentina explaining her vision and Bianca offering insights as to how to navigate the labyrinth of cultural preservation laws, and by the end of the day, they have formed an alliance.

Bianca's involvement brings much needed legitimacy to Florentina's project. She is going to help her secure grants and introduce her to historians and architects who share her passion. And together, they will plan a museum to house some of the treasures that Florentina discovered in the tunnels.

"It's the best way to showcase the history of the town while preserving its soul," she says.

The days roll on and the air is crisp and fragrant with the scent of wildflowers. Florentina wanders through the square watching as the labourers put the final touches on the museum, its freshly painted façade gleaming under the Sicilian sun. It was a hard fought victory and a triumph that is tempered by a growing unease.

Domenico Bellini's presence lingers like a shadow over Poggioreale. Rumours swirl that he has been approaching landowners, offering extravagant sums for small parcels of land. The prospect of easy money was tempting for many, especially those who have long since abandoned the town.

Florentina's brothers are in the community hall, their faces a mix of concern and frustration as she enters.

"Do you know what I heard this morning?" Antonio said, his voice sharp. "Bellini bought the vineyard on the northern edge of town. That land borders our restoration area."

Florentina frowned. "How did he manage that? I thought the owner refused to sell."

Marco sighs. "He refused at first but then Domenico offered double what it's worth. Maybe more."

Luca, leaning casually against a table shrugs. "Can you blame them? Most of those people have no reason to care about Poggioreale anymore. They are just trying to make a living."

Florentina turns on him, her voice tight with anger. "That's exactly what he is counting on, people giving up. But I won't let him take this town piece by piece."

Antonio crosses his arms. "You had better have a plan, Florentina, because if he keeps buying land, he will gain enough leverage to block everything we are trying to do."

In the midst of these developments, Florentina and Carlo's relationship reaches a new level. One evening, after a long day of work, he invites her to join him for a quiet dinner not far from the vineyard. The air is cool, the sky is ablaze with stars and the table is simple but thoughtful.

"You have been so focused on the town," Carlo says as he pours her a glass of wine, "but you haven't stopped to think about yourself."

Florentina smiles, touched by his concern.

"Poggioreale is a part of me. Thinking about it is like thinking about myself."

"I know," he says, his gaze steady. "But I don't want you to lose yourself. You have given so much already."

She reaches across the table and takes his hand. "It's worth it and so are the people who have stood by me."

"Like you," she says.

Their connection deepens in that moment, and a quiet understanding passes between them. Carlo leans in, and Florentina meets him halfway, and their kiss is soft but filled with promise.

But not all is peaceful. Domenico Bellini is not finished yet, and in the following weeks, rumours begin to spread of offers being made to even more of the previous residents.

Domenico's goal is clear: if he cannot buy Poggioreale, he will chip away at it piece by piece. Florentina confronts him and is determined to put an end to his interference.

"You are a meddling fool and poking your nose into something you are not even interested in," she says, her voice sharp.

Domenico smirks. "I understand opportunity, Signorina Grasso, and this town is full of it."

"It is full of memories and lives, and you cannot buy that."

"Can't I?" he says, his tone mocking. "We will see how long you can hold out. Everyone has their price."

Florentina gives him his marching orders and sends him on his way and is more determined than ever to protect this town, but she knows that this fight is far from over.

The months roll on, and every morning without fail, the summer sun casts a golden glow over Poggioreale, but Florentina's mood is anything but bright. The vineyard restoration has reached its final stage, and the first harvest is weeks away, a major milestone in her efforts to revive the town. Yet, Domenico Bellini's shadow looms larger than ever.

Rumours are spreading. Domenico had been circulating false claims that Florentina is secretly selling the treasures from the tunnels to fund her project. In the nearby towns, whispers of her supposed greed reaches the ears of potential supporters and threatens to undermine her progress.

Later that day, Florentina finds Luca near the vineyard, chatting amiably with a few of the farm workers. His easy-going demeanour, usually a source of comfort, now grates on her nerves. She pulls him aside, her frustration boiling over, and approaches, her jaw set.

"Luca, we need to talk," she said.

He turns to her, his carefree smile replaced by a guarded expression. "What is it now?"

"Domenico," she says bluntly. "I have heard that he has been speaking to you."

"He made an offer. It's nothing serious."

"Nothing serious?" Florentina says. "He is trying to turn you against me, Luca, and against everything we are building here."

Luca crosses his arms, his tone defensive. "He said he wants to invest in the town, to make it better. And let's be honest, Florentina, you can't do this alone or forever."

Her eyes narrow. "And you believe him? After everything we have seen him do?" "Domenico is trying to destroy everything we have worked for, and you are acting like it's some kind of game."

Luca hesitates, guilt flashing across his face.

"I don't want you to burn out, sorellina. You are carrying too much on your shoulders."

Florentina steps closer, her voice softening. "I am not doing this alone, Luca. I have all of my family with me, but if we let Domenico drive a wedge between us, we will lose everything."

Luca looks into her in the eyes, his jaw tightening. "I am with you, Florentina but I just hope you know what you are doing."

"Do you even understand what's at stake here?"

He raises an eyebrow. "Of course I do but getting worked up won't change anything."

Luca's smile fades, his tone growing defensive. "I am not the enemy here, Florentina. Maybe you should focus less on fighting and more on finding solutions."

Her eyes narrow. "If you are not with me, then you are making it easier for him."

The tension between them lingers as she storms off, but later that night, Florentina finds Luca near the vineyard, a bottle of wine at his side. She approaches cautiously, her anger tempered by concern.

"You have been quiet," she says, as she takes a seat at his side.

Luca takes a swig from the bottle, his gaze fixed on the horizon. "I am just trying to make sense of all of this."

"Of what?"

He sighs. "I didn't sign up for a war, Florentina. I thought we were rebuilding something beautiful, not tearing ourselves apart."

Her voice softens. "Luca, I know this is hard. But Domenico isn't just challenging me, he is challenging all of us. If we give up now, everything we have worked for will be lost."

Luca turns to her, his expression conflicted. "And what if we lose anyway?"

"Then we go down fighting," she says firmly. "Because this isn't just about a town. It's about who we are."

For a long moment, they sit in silence. Finally, Luca nods, his resolve strengthening. "Okay. I'm with you."

The following day, Domenico Bellini makes his next move. Florentina is reviewing plans in her grandfather's house when she hears a knock on the door. She opens it, only to find Domenico, his smile as disarming as ever.

"Good morning, Signorina Grasso," he says, his tone almost pleasant. "May I come in?"

Florentina steps outside and closes the door. "Whatever you have to say, you can say it here."

Domenico chuckles, spreading his hands in a gesture of feigned innocence. "No need to be so hostile. I am here to make you an offer."

"I am not interested."

"You haven't even heard it yet," he said, his voice smooth. "I will buy the entire town from you. Name your price."

Florentina's laugh is cold and sharp. "Do you think this is about money?"

"It's always about money," Domenico replies, his smile fading. "Be reasonable, Florentina. You are fighting a losing battle. Let me take this off your hands before it consumes you."

She steps up very close, her voice like hardened steel. "Poggioreale is my home. It is not a commodity to be traded. And if you think I will let you turn it into a playground for the wealthy, you don't know me at all."

For the first time, Domenico's polished veneer cracks, revealing a glimpse of the ruthlessness beneath. "Be careful, Signorina. Stubbornness can be costly."

"I will take my chances," she says, her gaze unwavering.

Domenico turns and walks away, his silhouette disappearing into the twilight, but his parting words hang in the air, a chilling reminder of the battle ahead.

CHAPTER 11

The Museum Opens

The day that Florentina has been working towards has finally arrived: the opening of Poggioreale's museum, housed in one of the town's restored villas, a two-story building with tall windows and a commanding view of the valley.

A collection of artifacts from homes and the tunnels are displayed alongside photographs and stories of the town's past, weaving a narrative that connects Poggioreale's history to its revival.

Despite the mounting challenges, Florentina presses on. The museum is a triumph, drawing visitors from neighbouring towns, and the square buzzes with excitement as locals and tourists marvel at the artifacts on display.

Locals mingle with visitors and the excitement is palpable. Journalists come from Palermo and beyond to cover the event, their cameras flashing as Florentina stands at the centre of the crowd, welcoming everyone.

Bianca Morretti stands at her side, dressed in a simple but elegant suit. "This is a moment of which to be proud. You have accomplished something extraordinary here," Bianca says, her tone warm but measured. "But I sense that there is more to this story than you are letting on."

Florentina hesitates before replying. "Domenico Bellini is trying to buy the town out from under me."

Bianca's expression darkens. "Bellini has a reputation and he won't stop until he gets what he wants."

"I won't let him win," Florentina says firmly. "Not after everything we have done."

Bianca places a hand on her shoulder. "Then you will need allies, and I will make sure that you have them."

Florentina smiles but she has a task ahead and steps up onto the makeshift stage to address the crowd.

"Today, we celebrate not just a museum but the resilience of a community. Poggioreale would have been lost and forgotten, but through your support, it is finding its voice again. "

"This museum is only the beginning, and together, we will continue to honour the past while building a future that we can all be proud of."

The crowd erupts in applause, and for a brief moment, Florentina allows herself to bask in the joy of the occasion.

As the sun set over Poggioreale, the square comes alive with music and laughter. Florentina watches from the sidelines, her heart swelling with pride despite the weight of her worries.

Carlo joins her, a glass of wine in hand. "It's a day to celebrate," he says, his voice steady.

"For now," she replies. "But Domenico isn't going to give up. He has already turned some of the locals against us."

Carlo's expression hardens. "Then we remind them of what this place means. You have already done the impossible, Florentina. Don't let him make you doubt yourself."

She looks at him, gratitude softening her features. "Thank you, Carlo. For everything."

They stand in silence, watching as the celebrations unfold. There will be challenges ahead, but this moment is a victory, a reminder of what's worth fighting for.

"May I have this dance?" he says as he extends his hand.

She laughs softly. "You have been waiting for the perfect moment, haven't you?"

"Always," he says with a grin.

They join other people on the makeshift dance floor, with the warm glow of lanterns overhead. As they move together, Florentina feels the weight of the past few years lifting, only to be replaced by a sense of hope and possibility.

CHAPTER 12

Domenico's Last Play

As Poggioreale's success grows, so does Domenico Bellini's frustration. His attempts to buy land have been met with resistance, thanks in part to Florentina's rallying of the local community, but Domenico is not a man who gives up easily. One afternoon, Florentina receives a letter from his lawyers informing her of his intent to file a claim against ownership of Poggioreale and alleging improper acquisition of certain parcels of land.

The letter is full of legal jargon but its message is clear: he intends to tie her up in court and hopes to exhaust her resources and her resolve.

Florentina reads the letter aloud to her brothers in her grandfather's house, and the room falls silent.

"It's a legal claim," she says, her voice taut. "Domenico is challenging my ownership of Poggioreale."

Antonio scans the document. "He is alleging fraud in the transfer of the deeds. He is saying that Nonno did not have the right to leave you the town."

Marco curses under his breath. "This is a power play. He knows that we do not have the resources for a prolonged legal fight."

Luca, sitting quietly at the edge of the table, looks troubled. "What if he is right? What if this becomes too big for us to handle?"

Florentina's snaps, her voice sharp.

"We have come too far to back down now Luca. Poggioreale is ours, Nonno made sure of that. Domenico is grasping at straws, and I am not going to let him win."

Carlo appears carrying a stack of papers. "Bianca sent these," he says. "She has already started documenting the restoration process and gathering evidence to counter his claims."

"Then we fight with whatever it takes," Florentina says.

"He is trying to intimidate us but he is bluffing," Antonio says.

"What if he isn't? A legal battle could drag on for years," Florentina says.

Luca leans back in his chair, his expression thoughtful. "We need a plan, something that will show him that we will not back down."

Florentina's mind is racing. "Bianca might know someone who can help. If Domenico wants a fight, we will give him one, but on our terms."

Bianca introduces her to a prominent lawyer, Alessia Conte, who specialises in historical preservation. Together, they prepare a defence and gather documents that prove her grandfather's ownership of Poggioreale and the legitimacy of her restoration efforts.

Bianca comes through with a plan to bypass Vizzini, rallying support from preservationists and historians who pressured the council to approve the permits. But Domenico's presence looms like a storm cloud. Rumours began to circulate that he is still buying up small plots of land in Poggioreale, attempting to gain a foothold in the town. Florentina knows that she will have to confront him eventually, but before that, she needs to secure her progress.

She turns to the community for support and organises a town meeting, inviting residents, workers, and supporters from neighbouring villages.

"We have come too far to let one man undo everything we have built," Florentina says, her voice steady but passionate. "Poggioreale is not land to be bought and sold. This is our home, and our history, and if we stand together, we can protect it."

The room erupts into applause, and people pledge their support. Some offer to testify on her behalf, while others volunteer to help spread the word about Domenico and his malicious scheme.

As the legal battle looms, Carlo becomes Florentina's anchor, and one evening, as they sit on the steps of the church, he takes her hand.

"You are not alone in this," he says. "Whatever happens, we will face it together."

She look him in the eyes, gratitude swelling in her heart. "I don't know what I would do without you."

"You won't have to find out," he says, his voice warm and unwavering.

The next few weeks are a whirlwind of preparation. Florentina's lawyer file counterclaims, accusing Domenico of attempting to coerce landowners and disrupt the restoration. Media coverage of the case turns public opinion sharply against Domenico, painting him as a villain trying to exploit Poggioreale's revival for personal gain.

A week later, Poggioreale gathers to celebrate the vineyard's first harvest in decades. The vines are heavy with grapes, their deep purple hue glinting in the sunlight. Workers move through the fields, their laughter mingling with the rhythmic snip of pruning shears.

In the square, long tables are set up for the evening feast. Florentina works tirelessly alongside her brothers, and Carlo ensures that every detail is perfect. The vineyard's revival is a testament to their perseverance, and she is determined to make the celebration a success.

As the sun dips below the horizon, the square comes alive with music and conversation. Locals and visitors raise their glasses to toast Poggioreale's future, their voices filled with hope.

Florentina stands before them, her glass held high. "This vineyard is more than just a harvest. It is a symbol of what Poggioreale can be, a place of growth, of resilience, and of community. Thank you all for believing in this dream."

But not long after, Antonio appears his expression grim.

"We have a problem," he said.

They head for the vineyard where several workers are gathered, murmuring in low tones. In the soft glow of lanterns, Florentina sees the damage: vines have been uprooted, grapes have been trampled, and the irrigation system has been sabotaged.

Her heart sinks. "When did this happen?"

"It must have been earlier today," Antonio said. "No one noticed until now."

Carlo arrives, his face dark with anger. "This wasn't an accident."

Florentina's fists clench at her sides. "It's Domenico, and he is sending a message." Despite the damage, she refuses to let him ruin the evening. She returns to the square, her determination unshaken.

"Should we call off the celebration?" Marco says, his voice low.

"No," Florentina says firmly. "That's exactly what he wants. We will deal with this tomorrow. Tonight, we celebrate what we have accomplished."

Her brothers agree and even Luca, standing at the edge of the square with a troubled expression, raises his glass in solidarity as Florentina catches his eye.

After the celebrations have wound down, Florentina gathers her brothers and Carlo in her grandfather's house. They sit around the kitchen table, the weight of the day pressing heavily on their shoulders.

"We need to hit back," Antonio says. "Domenico is playing dirty, and we can't afford to let him get the upper hand. If we stoop to his level, we will lose the moral high ground."

"Bianca is going to document every aspect of the restoration to prove our transparency. If Domenico wants a fight, we will give him one, in court."

"You are not alone in this,'" Carlo says. "We are with you."

Florentina's heart swells with gratitude. "Then we will show Domenico what Poggioreale is made of."

CHAPTER 13

The Final Hearing

On the day of the hearing, Florentina sits in the front row, flanked by her lawyer, Alessia Conte, and her brothers. Across the room, Domenico Bellini exudes his usual arrogance, his legal team flanking him like well-dressed vultures. The day has arrived, and Florentina feels the support of the townspeople on her shoulders.

As the judge enters, the room falls silent. This is the moment that will determine the future of Poggioreale.

Domenico's lawyer present what they claim is new evidence, a series of documents that purport to show irregularities in Pietro Grasso's acquisition of Poggioreale decades earlier.

"Your Honor," Domenico's lawyer says, "these records indicate that the deeds were transferred under false pretences. It calls into question the entire basis of Signorina Grasso's claim."

Over the next few days, the courtroom becomes a second home for Florentina, but each day brings a new challenge, from fabricated evidence to procedural delays orchestrated by Bellini's legal team. Yet, for every move Domenico makes, Alessia Conte has a counter move.

The courtroom is packed and the townspeople have turned out in droves, their presence a testament to the growing support for Florentina's fight. Bianca Morretti sits in the front row, her notebook open, ready to testify if needed. Carlo and her brothers sit by her side, each one offering silent encouragement.

Domenico's team presents their latest argument, claiming that Florentina illegally removed treasures from the tunnels, exploiting Poggioreale's history for personal gain.

Domenico's lawyer smirks. "Your Honor, this case is not just about ownership. It's about ethics. Signorina Grasso has systematically removed artifacts from Poggioreale, claiming them as her own."

Alessia stands up, her voice sharp. "Your Honor, the artifacts in question have been preserved and catalogued as part of Poggioreale's restoration. They are displayed in the town's museum for public education, with proper records of their origins."

She hands the documents over to the judge who flips through the pages.

Bianca testifies, her tone measured but firm. "As an expert in historical preservation, I can confirm that every artifact has been handled according to the law. The museum is a model of cultural integrity."

The smirk on Domenico's face falters as murmurs spread through the courtroom. His lawyer tries to change the subject but the damage has been done.

Alessia Conte is a sharp-witted woman who faces Domenico's legal team in a packed courtroom in Palermo. Domenico is flanked by a high-priced lawyer who exudes far too much confidence, his constant smirk, a taunt that Florentina refuses to acknowledge.

His voice is smooth and practiced. "Your Honor, the deeds in question are irregular at best. The previous owner, Pietro Grasso, failed to properly register the transfer, casting doubt on its validity."

Alessia rises, her tone cutting. "Your Honor, the deeds are legitimate. The papers are stamped and signed, which means that they are legitimate."

"The only irregularity here is Signor Bellini's baseless attempt to claim land that does not belong to him."

Alessia's voice sharp. "Your Honor, we request a recess to examine these documents. Their sudden appearance is highly suspicious."

The judge nods. "Granted. This court will reconvene in two hours."

In the conference room, Florentina, Alessia, and Bianca pour over the documents when Luca makes an appearance, his expression unreadable.

"Luca," Florentina says, surprised. "What are you doing here?"

He places a folder on the table. "I am making things right. I found these and I think they will come in very useful."

Inside the folder are the original copies of records from the local archives, records that contradict Domenico's forged documents. Luca spent the previous night digging through municipal files after overhearing one of Domenico's men bragging about "altering history."

"I know I messed up," Luca says, his voice quiet. "But I couldn't let him win. Not like this."

Florentina's eyes soften, her anger giving way to gratitude. "You have done more than make up for it, Luca. Thank you."

Alessia prepares the evidence, her energy renewed by the breakthrough. "This changes everything."

When court reconvenes, she presents Luca's findings. The original records not only confirm Pietro's legal acquisition of Poggioreale but also expose the discrepancies in Domenico's documents.

"Your Honor," Alessia says, as she hands the new evidence over to the judge. "These documents not only prove the legitimacy of Signorina Grasso's ownership but also highlight the fraudulent nature of the evidence presented by the plaintiff."

The judge examines the papers, his expression hardening. "Signor Bellini, do you have an explanation for this?"

Domenico's lawyer stumbles through a weak defence, but it's clear that the tide has turned. The judge calls for a recess, and when he returns, his verdict is swift.

"This court finds in favour of Signorina Grasso. The deeds to Poggioreale are valid, and the claims brought forth by Signor Bellini are dismissed as baseless."

The courtroom erupts into cheers, and Florentina turns to Alessia, tears of relief in her eyes. "We did it," she cries.

The news spreads quickly, and when Florentina finally gets back to Poggioreale, the square is filled with celebrating townspeople. They cheer as she steps out of the car, offering hugs and congratulations.

Bianca raises a glass, her voice carrying over the crowd. "To Florentina Grasso, the woman who saved Poggioreale."

The crowd roars in agreement, and an emotional Florentina stands on the museum steps, looking out at the faces of the people she fought for.

"This victory isn't just mine. It belongs to all of us. Poggioreale's future is bright because we stood together, because we believed in what this town could be. Thank you for your strength, your trust, and your love. This is only the beginning."

That evening as she looks out upon the celebrations Carlo appears at her side.

"How did it go?"

"It's not over yet," she says, as she leans in closely. "But Alessia was brilliant, and Bianca's testimony made an impact."

Carlo wraps an arm around her shoulder. "You will win, Florentina. I know you will."

"How can you be so sure?"

"Because I have seen what you are capable of."

In that moment, the weight of the battle lifts, only to be replaced by the quiet strength of their partnership.

CHAPTER 14

The Tourists Arrive

The transformation of Poggioreale has reached a tipping point, and after years of labour, the town is ready to welcome visitors from all over the world. The restored square, now bustling with a café and artisan shops are alive. The museum attracts the attention of historians and travellers alike, and word has spread far beyond Sicily.

The first tour group arrives on a warm spring morning, and a sleek bus rolls into the square, its passengers disembarking with cameras and eyes wide. Florentina stands at the edge of the square, her heart swelling with pride as she watches them explore.

An elderly woman approaches Florentina, her voice thick with emotion. "I grew up in a village not far from here, and seeing this is like stepping back into my childhood."

Florentina smiles, her voice gentle. "That's exactly what I hoped to create, a place where memories can live again."

"You have done something remarkable here, Signorina Grasso. Thank you."

The newly opened café in the square, run by a young couple from a neighbouring village offers traditional Sicilian pastries and strong espresso. Florentina sits at one of the outdoor tables with Carlo and watches as the scene unfolds.

"It feels surreal," she says as she takes a sip of her coffee. "All these people here, enjoying what we have built."

Carlo smiles, his hand resting over hers. "They are not just enjoying it; they are becoming a part of it. That's the magic of this place."

Their quiet moment is interrupted by Luca, who approaches the table. "You two look as if you are planning your next empire."

"Not an empire," Florentina replies "Just a legacy."

CHAPTER 15

Personal Milestones

As Poggioreale thrives, so does Florentina's personal life. Carlo is her partner in every sense and supports her vision, and all the while, they are quietly building a life of their own. One evening, after a long day at work, Carlo surprise her with a simple but heartfelt proposal.

The setting is the vineyard, bathed in the soft glow of sunset, and Carlo gets down on one knee and holds out a modest but beautiful ring.

"Florentina, you have rebuilt this town from ruins. And you have shown me what love, resilience, and hope look like. Now, I would like to build something with you."

"Will you do me the honour of marrying me?" he says.

Florentina catches her breath and tears well in her eyes. "Yes," she says, her voice trembling with emotion. A thousand times yes."

Carlo rises and takes her in his arms, and in the background, the vineyard sways gently in the breeze. In that moment, Florentina feels the weight of the past lifting, replaced by the promise of a bright and enduring future.

The news of their engagement spreads quickly, and a few days later, the town celebrates with the kind of fervour that only Sicilians can muster. The square is alive with music, dancing, and laughter as the community gathers to honour their future together.

As the years pass, their family grows, and they welcome their first child, a bright-eyed boy who they call Pietro in honour of Florentina's grandfather. As she watches her son toddle through the square, Florentina feels the full circle of life in Poggioreale, a town that was once silent but is now filled with the laughter of children.

Her brothers also find new roles in the revitalised town. Marco manages the logistics of a growing economy, overseeing the vineyards and new shops.

Antonio, always the realist, becomes the unofficial mayor, navigating politics and bureaucracy with a steady hand. And Luca, the eternal dreamer opens a workshop where people can craft dreams inspired by the town's historical origins. The culmination of Poggioreale's rebirth comes with its first major festival in decades. The Festa Della Rinascita (The Festival of Renewal) is held on the anniversary of the museum's opening and draws crowds from Sicily and beyond. Poggioreale is transformed, tables are set up, and villagers bustle about, preparing food and hanging lanterns between buildings. The townspeople have organized a celebration like no other.

"This was their idea," Bianca says, as she gestures at the scene. "They believe in you, Florentina."

Her throat tightens as she watches a group of children hang a banner that reads, *"Poggioreale is Our Home and Our History."*

"Sometimes I wonder if I deserve it," she says quietly.

Carlo places a hand on her shoulder. "You do. And so does this town."

The town square is transformed into a vibrant tapestry of colours and sounds. Market stalls offer fresh local goods, musicians play traditional tunes, and children run through the streets with sparklers in their hands. Florentina stands at the heart of it all, her family by her side.

As the fireworks light up the night sky, Florentina gazes out over the town. Carlo slips an arm around her waist, their three children at their side. Her family is nearby and raise their glasses in a toast.

Florentina smiles, her heart full. "We did it," she says softly, the words more to herself than anyone else.

Carlo kisses her on the cheek. "You did it, Florentina. You made your grandfather's dream come true."

As the last of the fireworks burst into the sky and paint the valley in hues of gold and red, Florentina feels a deep sense of peace. Poggioreale is no longer a memory frozen in time, it is alive and thriving, just as it was always meant to be.

CHAPTER 16

The Last Stone

The day of the final milestone in the restoration of Poggioreale has arrived, and the town's old clock tower, which has stood silent since the earthquake is ready to ring again.

Ever since the earthquake it has been a symbol of loss, its broken hands frozen in time. Now, as the workers make their final adjustments, it stands as a beacon of renewal.

Florentina climbs the narrow spiral staircase, her heart pounding with anticipation. At the top of the tower, Carlo is waiting, his hands steady on the controls of the new mechanism.

"Are you ready?" he says, his eyes bright with excitement.

Florentina nods, her voice filled with emotion. "Let's bring it back to life."

Carlo set the gears in motion, and for the first time in years, the hands of the clock begin to move. The bell rings out across Poggioreale, its rich tone echoing through the valley, and below, the crowd cheers loudly, their joy so very palpable. Florentina gazes out from the tower, the view of the restored town spreading before her. Cobblestone streets, vibrant shops, and the laughter of children fill the square. She feels a deep sense of fulfillment, knowing that they have achieved the impossible.

That evening, Florentina sits alone on her grandfather's porch, a glass of wine in hand. She looks out across the valley, its rolling hills bathed in moonlight. Her thoughts drift back to the journey that brought her here, the challenges, the triumphs, and the people who made it possible.

She opens a small box, and inside is her grandfather's letter, the one he left for her twenty years ago. She reads his words again, feeling their weight anew.

Poggioreale is not just a place. It's a story, one that belongs to all who remember it and all who will call it home again. You are its guardian, Florentina. Protect it, and it will give you more than you could ever imagine.

Tears fill her eyes as she whispers, "Thank you, Nonno for believing in me."

Carlo appears in the doorway, carrying their youngest daughter in his arms. "You are thinking about him, aren't you?" he says.

She nods smiling softly. "He would have loved this."

"And he would be so proud of you," Carlo says, as he places a hand on her shoulder. "Just as I am."

Carlo slips his arm around her waist, pulling her closer, and they gaze out over the valley that has been the heart of this journey.

"Do you ever think about the day you first came back here?" he says, his voice low.

"All the time," Florentina says. "I remember how empty it felt, how heavy the silence felt. I thought I would never hear life in this valley again."

"And now?" Carlo says, as she brushes a strand of hair from her face.

She looks at him, her heart full. "Now I hear laughter, music, the wind in the vines and I see everything I dreamed this place could be, and more."

Carlo smiles. "It's a good thing you're stubborn."

She laughs softly and rests her head against his shoulder. "It's a good thing I have you."

EPILOGUE

Poggioreale's Legacy
Twenty Years Later

The Grasso family gathers on the balcony in front of Nonno's house and gazes out over the town they brought back to life. Below them, Poggioreale sparkles with light and laughter, the square a testament to the resilience of its people. The distant hum of the vineyards, the chime of the clock tower, and the faint melody of a street musician blend into a symphony of life.

Carlo steps forward, his hand gently resting on Florentina's shoulder. The glow of the lanterns catch the warmth in his eyes as he turns to face her.

"You know," he says, his voice steady but filled with emotion, "it's as if an angel came down from above."

The Grasso family turn and listen to his every word.

"But it wasn't the usual sort of angel, not one cloaked in quiet serenity. No, this angel had fire in her eyes and conviction in her soul. She waved her wand, not to grant wishes, but to conjure the magic of belief in the hearts of everyone who dares to dream."

Florentina's cheeks are flushed and her eyes glistening as he speaks. "She didn't just restore this town. She gave it a heart and she reminded all of us that sometimes, all it takes is one person with a dream, and the courage to fight for it."

The silence is broken by gentle sobbing and a few stray tears. Antonio's expression is one of pride and respect. Marco and Lucia wipe a stray tear from their eyes, and even Pietro, who is usually stoic, smiles and raises his glass.

Luca, ever the showman, steps forward, and raises his glass with a flourish. "To my sister," he says, his voice loud and playful. "The angel with fire in her eyes and a stubborn streak that puts the rest of us to shame."

The family laughs, their spirits light. Luca gestures to the town below, the vineyard stretching beyond it like a sea of promise.

"But enough talk. I say we enjoy the fruits of our labour as we gaze out across the field of victory."

The group raise their glasses in unison, a chorus of agreement. "To Florentina and to Poggioreale."

Down below, where the lights shimmer like a constellation brought to earth, the town square is alive with joy, children darting through the crowd, families sharing stories, and visitors marvelling at the beauty of a place that might have been frozen in time.

The vineyards roll into the distance, their vines heavy with promise. The museum glows warmly, its doors open late to welcome those eager to learn the stories of the past. The clock tower, its chime steady and proud, stands as a sentinel over the town, a symbol of time reclaimed.

Carlo slips his arm around Florentina, leans close and whispers in her ear. "Look at what you have done, my angel."

Florentina, her voice soft but certain says, "Look at what we have done."

As the night deepens, the family lingers on the balcony, their laughter mingling with the sounds of the celebration below. Florentina glances at each of them, her steadfast brothers, her loving husband, her children who will carry this legacy forward, and she feels her heart swell.

This is more than she had dreamed of. Poggioreale isn't just alive, it is thriving. It's a beacon of resilience, love, and hope for everyone who dares to believe in the impossible.

And as they gaze out across the valley, hands intertwined and hearts full, Florentina knows that this is only the beginning of the story they have written together.

The clock tower strikes the hour, its chime carrying across the fields. Florentina closes her eyes, the sound, a melody of triumph. She whispers into the night, her words carried by the breeze.

"Thank you, Nonno for believing in me. We brought our home back to the world."

And as the lights of Poggioreale shine brighter than ever, a legacy has been reclaimed, and a dream fulfilled. It will become a destination known across Sicily and beyond. The town now draws tourists from around the world who come to experience its unique blend of history. Guided tours showcase the treasures of the tunnels, while the vineyards produce award-winning wines.

Florentina, now in her fifties often walks through the bustling square, greeting familiar faces and new visitors. Her children are grown and each one contributes to Poggioreale in their own way. Pietro, her eldest has taken over the operation of the vineyards while her daughter Lucia manages the museum.

As she strolls past the café, she overhears a group of tourists marvelling at the town's transformation.

"This place is incredible," one says. "It's like stepping into the past but it's alive."

Florentina's heart swells with pride and she heads for the church where Carlo is overseeing preparations for a festival. He waves when he sees her, his smile as warm as ever. They stand together at the edge of the square, watching as the clock in the tower chimes the hour. The sound carries across the valley, a reminder of how far they have come.

Florentina turns to Carlo, her voice quiet but full of gratitude. "Do you think Nonno ever imagined this?" she says.

Carlo takes her hand, his fingers entwining with hers. "He imagined you and that was enough."

Florentina looks out over Poggioreale. It is no longer a ghost town but a living testament to resilience, love, and the power of a dream.

THE END

CHAPTER 17

The Gods of Space and Time
A series of fantasy fiction stories.
THE ETERNAL OPTIMIST
BOOK ONE

Unlike his brother who is cautious and irritable, Addric has a bit of a reputation. He not only believes in miracles, he believes in the impossible.

Their holiday plans are sabotaged from the first day and they barely survive one life threatening situation after another. The stakes are high, and they have to succeed. A card-carrying member of the dark side is out to get his revenge, but they can't allow that to happen. Addric rises to the challenge and shows what he is made of.

He proves to everyone that he is both brilliant, and audacious. Fearless is a rollercoaster ride through an inter-dimensional realm, a place where unusual things can happen.

A drama set in motion long, long ago is about to unfold. All they wanted was a boy's own holiday. They had no idea what sort of holiday they were in for.

This story was selected as a finalist in The 2020 Book Excellence Awards.

THE OCEAN OF INFINITE MYSTERY
BOOK TWO

Allow your mind to roam further than it has ever done before, to the outer perimeter of Alpha Centauri. It is here you will find a galaxy called the Khavala, an inter-dimensional realm, where many worlds exist side-by-side, a world of strange beauty, hidden power, and wondrous mystery.

The Khavala is a self-conscious entity, but when danger threatens the most sacrosanct of all domains, she calls upon the assistance of her most powerful creations, an invincible task force that includes Yumi Masters, and Warrior Angels.

To resolve this problem, they must travel deep into the heart centre of the Khavala, to a place of legend, to the domain known since time immemorial as The Ocean of Infinite Mystery.

THE LAST DAYS OF LEMURIA
BOOK THREE

Elisabeth Trundle's life changes on the day that she meets two attractive young men in The Great Library of London, but these guys are not Earthlings as she eventually finds out.

Elisabeth has been having dreams about the lost continent of Lemuria, but the last thing she expected is that she would actually get an opportunity to go there. And that would never have happened if the chronometer of a passing spaceship had not malfunctioned.

Accompanied by four Yumi Masters, Elisabeth's dream comes true, and she ends up in a civilisation that is about to be destroyed by a natural catastrophe.

Over the next two weeks, they have to train an army, defeat the high priest at his own game and save a young boy's life.

But it's not all bad news, the people are wonderful, and the food is even better. Before the dreaded day dawns, they discover how the Lemurians intend to survive.

THE GOLDEN PHOENIX
BOOK FOUR

Accompanied by a few feisty friends, Addric embarks on a mission to rescue his brother's girlfriend from the clutches of a necromancer with delusions of grandeur.

To save Elisabeth, they will have to battle it out in the Roman arena, cross the Arctic Ocean on a crystal powered boat, venture deep into the bowels of the Earth, and then brave the fires of hell on a volcanic planet on the verge of a major transformation.

It will take something more than sharp claws and attitude to defeat a necromancer at his own game, but these boys are Yumi Masters, and they have a few tricks up their sleeve.

SAYONARA PLANET EARTH
BOOK FIVE

The people of Earth have become obsessed with electronic devices, but if they want to survive, they have to make the biggest sacrifice of all. The big guys upstairs are willing to give them one more chance, but only if they change their ways.

Yumi Master, Addric Sharano, has been assigned the task of dragging them back from the brink. Unfortunately, there is a time limit on this deal. Addric spearheads a team of people who use every trick in the book.

Earthlings are about to find out that not all aliens have a bulbous head and big green eyes. Sit back and enjoy the ride as Addric reveals a few of his hidden talents.

QUIETLY THEY CAME
BOOK SIX

Yumi Master extraordinaire, Addric Sharano is back, and he is in fine form in this light-hearted adventure. Addric's new mission is to rescue forty-two orphans from Pompeii, before they are incinerated by the volcano.

Accompanied by his best friends and glamorous offsiders, Lady Felicity, and her sister, Countess Demetra, two exponents of the fine old art of subterfuge, and the modern version of sorcery, Addric comes up with a clever if not complicated plan.

However, there is one little catch. These kids have a greater purpose in life. They were born with a coded message in their DNA, and it is just waiting for an opportunity to be expressed.

Addric is not known as the master of spin for nothing, so, he takes the kids by the hands, and they dive into the deep end. And when they come up for air, they hit the big time.

Addric is the man with golden touch when it comes to doing the impossible, and he doesn't fail to deliver the goods in this rollicking romp of a story. Sit back and enjoy a ride that starts in Pompeii and ends on some of the great stages of the modern world.

TEACH ME HOW TO FLY
BOOK SEVEN

The future of an inconspicuous village is threatened by an ungodly invader, but a prophecy states that a messiah will come to their rescue.

The first person on the scene is a Yumi Master with a history of battling the bad guys. And not long after, the real messiah appears in a blaze of glory.

Disposing of the invaders is a serious business, but they have quite a few tricks up their sleeve, and the most potent weapon in their armoury is the power of sound. And when they are not doing that, they entertain the musically inclined villagers with a selection of inspirational songs from the 20th century.

OTHER BOOKS
A PRAYER FOR BROTHER WILLIAM

After he loses his parents, William Cahill, retreats into a world of his own and his life would have spiralled out of control if it had not been for Aunt Augusta. She drags him back from the brink and transforms his life and that of his siblings, but Augusta Cahill is no ordinary woman.

She might be dreadfully wealthy and a pathetic old socialite, but she can be a force to be reckoned with. A story about life, death and suffering on the home front, a place that can be as perilous as a battlefield.

This novel, which is both historical fiction and a romance is also a tender portrayal of love in some of its myriad forms. It was inspired by an old family legend and is a story that breathes life into a bygone era with vivid authenticity.

THE SNAKE CHARMER'S TALE
Also published as
KASHMIRA:
THE SNAKE CHARMER'S WIFE

An enchanting tale set in 19th century Ceylon and 21st century Australia. A shipwreck off the coast of Ceylon. A diary that hold a key to a long-lost treasure. A tale that spans two continent and two centuries.

After discovering a diary written by a snake charmer called Roshan in 1884, Jasper Powell finds himself in the middle of an age old mystery.

As he unravels the story, Jasper uncovers a key to a treasure that has been stored away in an inconspicuous inner-city Melbourne building for over one hundred years.

Jasper realises that he has a treasure of cultural and historical significance on his hands and decides to make Roshan's dream a reality.

A tale that is rich with vivid characters and exotic lands, The Snake Charmer's Tale is a journey of natural and supernatural delights, interwoven with holy men, magic and miracles.

As one reader has said, this story is 'Simply Amazing.'

THE GODDESS OF GOOD FORTUNE
The Sequel to The Snake Charmer's Tale

When she is offered the opportunity to dispose of a recalcitrant necromancer, the illustrious Lady Felicity Originalis jumps at the chance. Lady Felicity is not your everyday detective. In fact, she is not a detective at all. She is an exponent of the fine old art of subterfuge, and the modern version of sorcery.

Felicity uses every trick in the book to protect a 9th century Arabian knight from the clutches of an evil Vizier. Memphalut el Shakar is the quintessence of a self-obsessed despot with the sharp but beady eyes of a pack hound.

Old-fashioned methods of torture are never on the agenda for Lady Felicity. She prefers to use other much more subtle forms of persuasion.

A TALE OF AN ARABIAN KNIGHT

In the fabled city of Aggrabad, nestled in the Rub al-Khali Desert, a tale of epic proportions unfolds. This lost city of the Bedouins, likened to the Atlantis of the Desert, is a masterpiece of glistening white limestone, a freshwater oasis, shrouded in mystery and romance.

At the heart of this story stands Hakim, the noble Captain of the Guards, who finds himself caught in a web of intrigue and sorcery woven by a tyrannical Sultan and the wicked Vizier, Memphalut al Shikari.

The Vizier, a practitioner of the dark arts rules through fear and cruelty, disposing of his enemies in the most horrific ways. Hakim and his fearless girlfriend, Zenobia must do everything in their power to make sure that the plans of this evil Vizier never come to pass.

I WILL BE PRAYING FOR YOUR SOUL

This story follows the journey of a cruel, violent and troubled soul, Justin Valéry, a twelve-year-old boy who torments everyone including his sister Majella and his family. After a terrifying experience in a church in Madrid, Justin mysteriously disappears, and finds himself in an alternate reality. He meets a mysterious man who informs him that he must embark on a journey of atonement and redemption. Justin undergoes a series of strange and challenging experiences in equally challenging environments and is forced to confront the consequences of his actions.

THE PASSIONFRUIT HOTEL

In a world where the culinary elite reign supreme, a tantalizing tale of revenge, betrayal, and supernatural intervention unfolds. At the heart of this delectable drama is Susannah Velasnikov, a Contessa whose life takes an unexpected turn when her good-for-nothing brothers meet an untimely demise. She reinvents herself with a new life as the proprietress of The Passionfruit Hotel, but things take a turn for the worst when she becomes embroiled in a web of shady dealings and ill-fated entanglements with the notorious Lord Alfred Chili Pepper.

MASTERMINDS OF MISCHIEF

Karim and Lucia are culinary ninjas, stealthy, cunning, and not to be messed with. They are the guardians of gastronomy, and Knights of the Kitchen. The Culinary Cabal holds the fate of the gastronomic world in their hands, but they are about to cook up a storm, inspired by a treasure trove of ancient herbs and spices.

In the world of culinary espionage, one false move and they could find themselves in the soup. A battle in the trenches of gourmet warfare is about to begin, and they have a world to save, one recipe at a time, before the Cabal can turn it into a pre-packaged nightmare.

Saving the world, one recipe at a time. It's about freedom, it's about creativity, it's about saving the culinary world. Don't even think about a future where every meal is a microwave tragedy

MERLIN'S SCHOOL
FOR ASPIRING LIGHTWORKERS
DESTINY CALLS

The lush rainforests of North Queensland is the stage for Merlin's School for Aspiring Lightworkers. A fantastical tale of magic, cosmic education, and the transformation of a group of teenagers into powerful lightworkers.

At the heart of the story is Marlin Martin, aka, Merlin, of great fame and acclaim, disguised as a 24-year-old man on a mission. This is a story that conveys a message of hope, transformation, and the power of individuals to create positive change, guided by the wisdom and magic of the legendary Merlin Ambrosius.

MERLIN'S SCHHOL OF MAGIC AND MYSTERY
THE SORCERER'S APPRENTICE

In a secluded valley deep in the mist-shrouded mountains, an ancient castle stands as a bastion of arcane knowledge and metaphysical mysteries. This is Merlin's School of Magic and Mystery, where the legendary sorcerer has gathered students from all over 6th century Britain.

Among the chosen few is Alistair Thorne, a bright-eyed youth from a small village who has always felt a deep connection to the unseen forces of the universe. His abilities set him apart from his peers, but they also attract Merlin's attention, thereby earning him a coveted place in the hallowed halls of the school.

Alistair crosses the threshold into a realm of wonders, and under Merlin's watchful eye, he and his enigmatic friends delve into the secrets of the cosmos and the primal energies that flow through all living things

This story is a whirlwind of ancient rituals, and mind-bending incantations, one in which Alistair is swept up into a deadly game that will test his courage and push him beyond the limits as a sorcerer's apprentice.

THE THRILL OF THE UNKNOWN

In the summer of 2024, a struggling German publisher, Marianna Bekendorpe finds an ancient book in a bookstore in Paris, one that transports her into a 6th-century tale about a young magician called Alastair Thorne, a protégé of the famous mage, Merlin Ambrosius.

Accompanied by his five best friends, Alastair embarks on a journey to spread the word that magic is the birthright of all. And wherever they go, they inspire hope, and sometimes skepticism.

This story, which has been lost for centuries, resurfaces in Marianna's hands. And with the assistance of her talented production team, she transforms this tale and republishes it with a different title.

Marianna's company desperately needs a best seller, and she is taking a big risk with this story. But she is hoping that this wonderful tale will find its way into the hearts of a modern-day audience. And if it does, her publishing company will finally become a global success.

Don't miss out!

Visit the website below and you can sign up to receive emails whenever VINCENT GILVARRY publishes a new book. There's no charge and no obligation.

https://books2read.com/r/B-A-XYCOC-DASIF

BOOKS 2 READ

Connecting independent readers to independent writers.

Did you love *Frozen in Time*? Then you should read *The Thrill of The Unknown*[1] by VINCENT GILVARRY!

In the summer of 2024, a struggling German publisher, Marianna Bekendorpe finds an ancient book in a bookstore in Paris that transports her into a 6th-century tale about a young magician called Alastair Thorne, a protégé of the famous mage, Merlin Ambrosius.

Accompanied by his five best friends, Alastair embarks on a journey to spread the word that magic is the birthright of all. Wherever they go, they inspire hope, and sometimes skepticism. This odyssey teaches them that true magic lies within.

This story, which has been lost for centuries, resurfaces in Marianna's hands. And with the assistance of a talented production team, she transforms this tale and republishes it as, "A Magical Mystery Tour."

Marianna's company desperately needs a best seller, and she is taking a big risk, and hoping that this wonderful tale finds its way into the hearts of a modern audience. And if it does, her publishing house will finally be a global success.

---

1. https://books2read.com/u/bMqnNk

2. https://books2read.com/u/bMqnNk

Read more at https://vgilvarry.blog/.

Also by VINCENT GILVARRY

Merlin's School for Aspiring Lightworkers
Destiny Calls

Merlin's School of Magic and Mystery
The Thrill of The Unknown

Standalone
I Will Be Praying For Your Soul
Masterminds of Mischief
Fun and Games at The Passionfruit Hotel
Merlin's School of Magic and Mystery
Frozen in Time

Watch for more at https://vgilvarry.blog/.

About the Author

Vincent Gilvarry is a writer from tropical North Queensland in Australia, a multifaceted author with a rich and vivid imagination.

With a foundation in the visual arts, his transition into the realm of literature was sparked by a life-changing situation that inspired him to embark on a literary career and an odyssey that has lasted for over 25 years.

He boasts an eclectic repertoire that highlights his versatility across various genres and his fantasy fiction books in particular are a testament to his unparalleled imagination and to his narrative prowess.

Read more at https://vgilvarry.blog/.

About the Publisher

Vincent Gilvarry is a writer from tropical North Queensland in Australia, a multifaceted author with a rich and vivid imagination.

With a foundation in the visual arts, his transition into the realm of literature was sparked by a life-changing situation that inspired him to embark on a literary career and an odyssey that has lasted for over 25 years.

He boasts an eclectic repertoire that highlights his versatility across various genres and his fantasy fiction books in particular are a testament to his unparalleled imagination and to his narrative prowess.

Read more at https://vgilvarry.blog/.

Milton Keynes UK
Ingram Content Group UK Ltd.
UKHW042145031224
452078UK00004B/481